Bunny & the Beast

retold by Molly Coxe

paintings by Pamela Silin-Palmer

Random House 🏠 New York

Acknowledgments

The artist gratefully thanks John Diamond, agent and friend;
Mallory Loehr, children's book editor; and Jan Gerardi, art director;
for their support and inspiration in creating this book.

www.randomhouse.com/kids

Library of Congress Cataloging-in-Publication Data

Coxe, Molly. Bunny and the beast / retold by Molly Coxe ;
illustrated by Pamela Silin-Palmer. p. cm. Summary: Through her great
capacity to love, a kind and beautiful rabbit maid releases a handsome
rabbit prince from the spell that has made him an ugly beast.

ISBN 0-375-80468-4

[1. Fairy tales. 2. Folklore—France.] I. Silin-Palmer, Pamela, ill. II. Title.
PZ8.C8395 Bu 2001 [398.2 09444 0452932]—dc21 99-048621

Printed in Singapore February 2001
10 9 8 7 6 5 4 3 2 1

To my dearest Patrick, to darling Jane,
and to Jack, a handsome and extremely busy bull terrier
—PS-P

To Mallory, who has lots of bonnes idées
—MC

Once upon a time, there was a rich rabbit merchant who had three daughters. The two oldest daughters, Thistle and Thorna, shopped all day long and ran up huge bills. But the youngest daughter was different. She loved reading, drawing, dancing, and watching things grow and change. Her name was Bunny.

One day, the merchant received terrible news. All of his ships had sunk in a storm at sea!

"I am ruined!" the merchant cried. "We will have to leave the city and live a simple life in the country."

"Get my paws dirty?" shrieked Thistle. "Never!"

"Hang out with hares?" howled Thorna. "I don't *think* so!"

"I will miss it here," Bunny said calmly. "But at least we will be together."

And so their city home was sold and the family moved to a cottage on the edge of a forest.

Bunny learned to cook and mend and tend a vegetable garden. She grew herbs and lavender and sold them in the small town nearby.

Thistle and Thorna didn't lift a paw to help. "Bunny doesn't seem to mind hard work, so she can do our share," they said.

A year passed, and the merchant got word that one of his lost ships had returned.

"I must leave for the city," the merchant said to his daughters. "Can I bring you anything?"

"Satin gowns!" Thistle ordered.

"Silk slippers!" Thorna commanded.

"Only a rose," Bunny said with a smile, "if it's not too much trouble."

"I will do my best," said the merchant, and he set off down the path.

In the city, the merchant was met with bad news. His only ship was wrecked, the cargo was lost, and the crew was demanding wages. The merchant paid them from his meager savings. All he had left were a few coins—not even enough for a rose.

The merchant was so upset when he left the city that he didn't notice he was lost in the forest until the road had disappeared. He was wandering aimlessly when he caught the smell of roasting vegetables. Following his nose, he found himself before a castle with golden light pouring through its open door. The merchant hopped in. He peeked into a grand room and saw a table covered with platters of hot food.

Someone must be ready to dine. When he arrives, I will ask him for a bite to eat, the merchant said to himself.

He sat down to wait. He waited for a long time. Finally, he was so hungry he took one little nibble, then another. Before he could stop, he had eaten everything in sight.

I must thank my host, the merchant thought as he fell asleep.

In the morning, the merchant woke in a fine bed with linen sheets the color of new grass. A silver tray with steaming oatmeal, jasmine tea, and fresh carrot juice floated in. Alarmed but hungry, he gobbled his breakfast, grabbed his bag, and was out the door. Hopping across the courtyard, he smelled roses and remembered Bunny's request! He stopped to pluck the perfect rosebud when…a thunderous growl shook the blossoms. "WHO DARES STEAL A ROSE FROM MY GARDEN?"

The merchant froze.

An enormous beast stepped out from behind a rosebush. His eyes were angry, his teeth were sharp, and his claws were long. But he was wearing a beautiful velvet suit.

"It is only I, a p-p-poor merchant," the merchant stammered.

"The same merchant I saved and fed and sheltered?" the Beast demanded.

"I meant no harm," pleaded the merchant. "The rose was to be a gift."

"A gift for whom?" asked the Beast.

So the merchant told the Beast of his daughters and his misfortunes. When he finished, the Beast said, "I will spare your life—on the condition that one of your daughters takes your place."

"Never!" said the merchant. "If you must devour someone, devour me!"

The Beast scowled. "If I were merely hungry, I would have eaten you already. Go home. One of your daughters must appear in a week, or I will destroy all of you. Leave now! Any path you choose will take you home." Then the Beast turned and was gone.

The merchant leapt about the forest until he found a path. As the Beast had promised, it led right to his doorstep, where Bunny was planting flowers.

Sadly, the merchant gave the rosebud to Bunny.

"Oh, Father, it's lovely," she said. "Where did you find it?"

"Where are my presents?" demanded Thistle from the doorway.

"They must be in his bag!" said Thorna. She tore open the bag and found satin gowns, silk slippers, and sparkling jewels.

Surprised, the merchant told his daughters everything—including the fact that the gowns, slippers, and jewels must have come from the castle. Last of all, he told them of his promise to the Beast.

"*I'm* not going," snapped Thistle, "even if this Beast *does* give nice presents."

"Bunny should go," sulked Thorna. "*She* wanted the rose that got you into this mess."

"I *will* go," Bunny said quietly, patting her father's paw.

Early in the morning, when the moon was still up, Bunny hopped silently out of the house. A shower of rose petals fluttered from the sky and settled on the ground before her. Bunny bravely walked along the petal path into the dark shadows of the forest.

At last she came to the shining castle of the Beast. The petal path led right up to the door!

$\mathcal{B}$unny pushed the heavy door open. There was a fire in the huge fireplace and a table set for breakfast. Bunny sat down. A silver tray flew in with peach nectar, clover pancakes, and broccoli flowers— Bunny's favorites!

Bunny calmly said, "Thank you," and nibbled her breakfast. When she was finished, she went to look around the castle. She discovered many rooms filled with magnificent furniture, tapestries, and more books than she'd ever seen. On the second floor, Bunny found a door with her name carved into it. She opened the door and stepped into an elaborate bedroom complete with a closet full of dresses and shoes in all the colors of the rainbow. A gorgeous gown covered with jewels danced out of the closet.

"For me?" asked Bunny. "You are beautiful, but a simple dress is better for daytime."

Quick as a wink, the fancy dress flew back into the closet, and out whisked a little silk dress embroidered with wildflowers.

"I love flowers!" said Bunny. "I just don't know how I can thank you enough— whoever you are!"

Bunny happily donned the new dress, then skipped outside to explore the castle grounds.

$\mathcal{B}$unny walked past formal gardens, sparkling fountains, and trellises hung with roses. There were winding paths, exotic trees, and fields of vegetables and flowers. There was even a little stream filled with goldfish.

When the sun began to set, Bunny hurried back to her room. Hot water and towels waited for her on the dressing table. A fresh golden dress hung on the closet door. Quickly, Bunny washed and changed. Then she hopped downstairs to the dining room.

The table was set for one, but there were two chairs.
As Bunny sat down, she heard heavy footsteps. She took a
deep breath and looked at the doorway. There was the Beast.
"Good evening, Bunny," he said. Unlike his appearance,
the Beast's voice was not terrible at all. "Do you need anything?" he asked.
"There *is* one thing," Bunny said timidly. "I left home without saying
good-bye to my father. He'll be worried about me."
"I have already sent him a message," the Beast said.

"Why, you are very kind!" said Bunny, surprised.

The Beast looked pleased with her compliment. He took the seat across from Bunny as platters of food began drifting onto the table.

"Help yourself," he said. "I never eat in front of others."

While Bunny ate, the Beast entertained her with amusing stories.

"I never thought you would be so interesting," Bunny said.

"Then . . . will you marry me?" asked the Beast.

Bunny's ears quivered. "I could never marry you," she said.

"Then I am doomed," said the Beast, and he left Bunny alone to ponder his words.

The next morning, Bunny woke to the smell of peppermint tea. She ate breakfast and went down to the castle library. She found some books she liked and spent her day reading in the gardens.

At dinner, Bunny hoped the Beast wasn't still upset. But when he came to the dining room, he was smiling. He asked her about her day, and she told him what books she had read. He had read them, too, and they talked about their favorite parts.

"Do you like to dance?" he asked after Bunny finished dessert.

"Oh, yes!" said Bunny.

"Follow me," said the Beast, and he led the way to the ballroom.

The minute Bunny entered, the air filled with splendid music. The Beast took Bunny's soft paw in his rough claw and danced with her as the sky filled with stars.

"Give me a chance," the Beast whispered into Bunny's long ear. "You might even love me someday."

Bunny looked away. She hated to hurt his feelings again, but she had to tell the truth. "I will stay here, but I will never love you," she said.

Yet every night after that, they danced in the ballroom . . .

. . . and walked in the moonlit gardens . . .
. . . and talked about books.
Every night, the Beast asked Bunny
to marry him. Every night,
her answer was no.

$\mathfrak{M}$onths passed. Bunny was happy, but she missed her home. Finally, she asked the Beast if she could go visit her father.

"Only for a short time," she promised. "Then I'll return."

"How can I be sure you'll come back?" the Beast said.

"Because I *want* to," said Bunny.

"Does this mean you'll marry me?" asked the Beast.

"No," said Bunny with a sigh. "I like you a lot, but I do not love you. I cannot marry you. You are a beast, after all, and I am a bunny."

The Beast looked at Bunny with tears in his eyes. "Go," he said. "This ring will take you to your father's house. Return in one week or I shall die."

"Of course," said Bunny. She kissed the Beast on the cheek and slipped the ring onto her finger.

The next instant, Bunny was home. She ran and hugged her father. Then she told him everything that had happened.

"The Beast has treated us kindly, too," said the merchant thoughtfully. "He sent us a chest full of gold soon after you left."

"And Thistle and Thorna?" said Bunny. "How are they?"

"They have married and moved away." He smiled and patted Bunny's paw. "I am content here and now my happiness is complete."

"Oh, Father," said Bunny. "I must return in one week."

"The Beast won't let you stay with me?" asked the merchant.

"It's not just *his* doing," replied Bunny. "He is my best friend. I would be sad never to see him again." She hugged her father again. "But, oh, how I've missed *you!*"

Seven days passed quickly. Just as Bunny was about to leave, Thistle and Thorna and their many babies came for a visit. They begged Bunny to stay and help with the children. *One day can't hurt,* thought Bunny, for she had forgotten the Beast's last words.

That night, she told her sisters about her life.

"This Beast is generous to *you!*" said Thistle. "But what about *us?* We haven't gotten a thing since the chest of gold."

"Yes!" said Thorna. "An ugly beast doesn't deserve to have so much."

Suddenly, Bunny saw her sisters in a different light. "That's not true!" she said. "The Beast may not be handsome, but he is kind and clever. You two are the *real* beasts! All you care about is money and clothes!" At that moment, she recalled the Beast's parting words. "I must go!" she gasped. "I only hope I am not too late!" She kissed her father good-bye and slipped the ring on.

The next second, she was in the castle gardens.
"Beast, where are you?" Bunny called. She ran
frantically from garden to garden, searching for him.
At last she found the Beast lying by the edge of the
stream. He held a rose in his claws, against his heart.
Bunny knelt down beside him.
"Oh, Beast, please don't die!" she pleaded.

Slowly, he opened his eyes.
"I was afraid you weren't coming,"
he whispered.

"I am here! I will stay with
you forever, dear Beast," said
Bunny, "as your wife, if you will
have me."

As soon as Bunny spoke these words, the Beast changed into a handsome rabbit prince, who sat up and took her paw. "Many years ago, a powerful enchantress turned me into a beast for being selfish and mean," he said. "The spell would endure until the day I had changed enough for someone to want to be with me, despite my looks. Before you came along, I never thought I could be different. Thank you for everything."

Bunny touched her nose to the Prince's. "You have always behaved like a prince to me," she declared. "I learned to love the goodness inside you, and now I think that you are devastatingly handsome as well!"

The wedding was held the very next day. Everyone in the kingdom came—even Thistle and Thorna. They behaved in their usual beastly fashion, but nothing could spoil Bunny and the Prince's joy.

They had a large, lovely family and lived happily ever after.